For Jason, my forever friend
~CF
For Anna, with all my love
~BC

Text Copyright © 2007 by Claire Freedman
Illustration Copyright © 2007 by Ben Cort
Published by arrangement with Simon & Schuster UK Ltd
1st Floor, 222 Gray's Inn Road, London, WC1X 8HB
A CBS Company

Dual language text copyright © 2011 Mantra Lingua
Audio copyright © 2011 Mantra Lingua
This edition 2011 All rights reserved
A CIP record for this book is available from the British Library
Mantra Lingua, Global House, 303 Ballards Lane, London, N12 8NP

www.mantralingua.com

Hear each page of this talking book narrated in many languages
with TalkingPEN! Then record your own versions.

Touch the arrow below with the TalkingPEN to start

Start   Info   English   Language

المخلوقات الفضائية تحب السراويل الداخلية

Aliens Love Underpants

Claire Freedman & Ben Cort

Arabic translation by Wafa' Tarnowska

Mantra Lingua

المخلوقاتُ الفضائيةُ تحبُ السراويلَ الداخلية من كلِ الأشكالِ والألوان ْ .
لكن لا توجدُ سراويلَ في الفضاء لذلك وجودها على الارضِ مفاجأة احياناْ ...

Aliens love underpants,
Of every shape and size.
But there are no underpants in space,
So here's a big surprise...

عندما تطيرُ المخلوقاتُ الفضائيةُ نحوَ الأرض ، لا تأتي لمقابلتك أنتَ ...
إنها تريد فقط سراويلك الداخلية ـ أراهنْ أنك لم تكن تعلمْ !

When aliens fly down to Earth, they don't come to meet YOU...
They simply want your underpants - I'll bet you never knew!

ان رادارَ مركبتهم الفضائية يضيء ويومضْ عندما يرىْ
حبلَ غسيلٍ ترفرفُ عليه سراويلَ داخلية في الهوا.

Their spaceship's radar bleeps and blinks the moment that it sees
A washing line of underpants all flapping in the breeze.

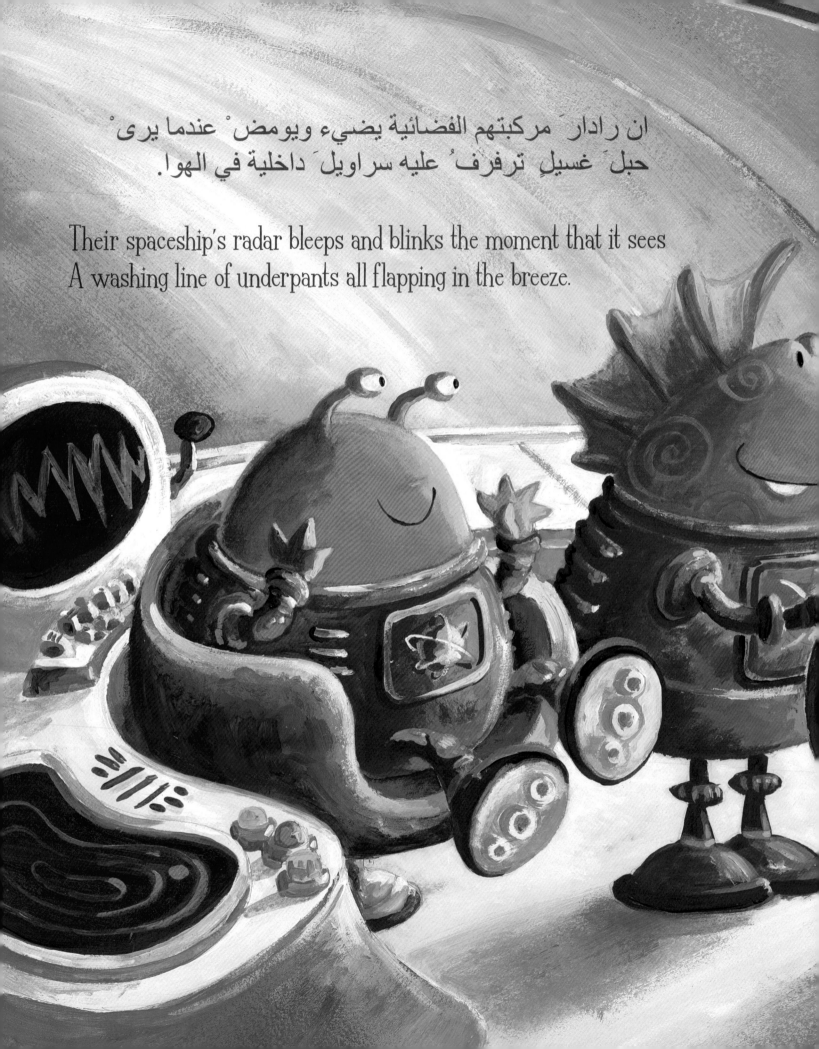

يهبطونَ في حديقتكَ الخلفية مع أنهم ليسوا مدعوونْ .
" آه ، سراويل داخلية ! " يغنونَ ، ويرقصونَ فرحونْ .

They land in your back garden, though they haven't been invited.
"Oooooh, UNDERPANTS!" they chant, and dance around, delighted.

يحبونها حمراء ويحبونها خضراء أو برتقالية كلون ِ الأفندي.
ولكنهم يحبونَ قبلَ كل ِ شيءٍ سراويلَ جدتي المنقطة بالبنفسجي.

They like them red, they like them green, or orange like satsumas.
But best of all they love the sight of Granny's spotted bloomers.

إن سراويلَ أمي الزهرية المزخرفة لمكانٌ ممتازٌ كي تختبىء ْ .
وسراويلُ جدي الطويلة الصوفية تشكل ُ زلاقة ً سريعة ً كي تنزلق ْ .

Mum's pink frilly knickers are a perfect place to hide
And Grandpa's woolly longjohns make a super-whizzy slide.

In daring competitions, held up by just one peg,
They count how many aliens can squeeze inside each leg.

في المسابقاتِ الجريئةِ والسراويلُ معلقةٌ
بملقطٍ واحدْ.
يعدونَ كم كائنٍ يمكنُ أن يختبأَ في ساقِ
سروالٍ واحدْ.

يضعون السراويل على رجليهم ورأسهم وأماكن أخرى سخيفة .
ويعلقون السراويل على مركباتهم الفضائية متسابقين على ايديهم العجيبة .

They wear pants on their feet and heads and other silly places.
They fly pants from their spaceships and hold Upside-Down-Pant Races!

بينما يطيرون في الفضاء، محلّقين، فرحين،
مشلين بمطاطات السراويل وسروليين.

As they go zinging through the air,
it really is pants-tastic.
What fun the aliens can have
with pingy pants elastic!

عندما تختفي السراويلُ لا تلومَ كلبَ الجيرانِ أو ألاعيبهم المرحةْ.
من الأفضلِ أن تلومَ المخلوقات الفضائية المازحة .

It's not your neighbour's naughty dog, or next-door's funny game.
When underpants go missing, the ALIENS are to blame!

But quick! Mum's coming out to fetch the washing in at last.
Wheee! Off the aliens all zoom, they're used to leaving fast...

هلموا ! ها هي أمي تلمُ الغسيلَ الناشفَ أخيراً .
واوْ ! هربتِ المخلوقاتُ الفضائيةُ بلحظةٍ ، سريعاً .

So when you put your pants on, freshly washed and nice and clean,
Just check in case an alien still lurks inside, unseen!

لذلك عندما تريدُ أن ترتدي سروالك النظيفَ ، المغسول ، المكويْ ،
لا تنسى أن تتفحصهُ لعل اختبأ فيهِ مخلوقٌ فضائيْ .